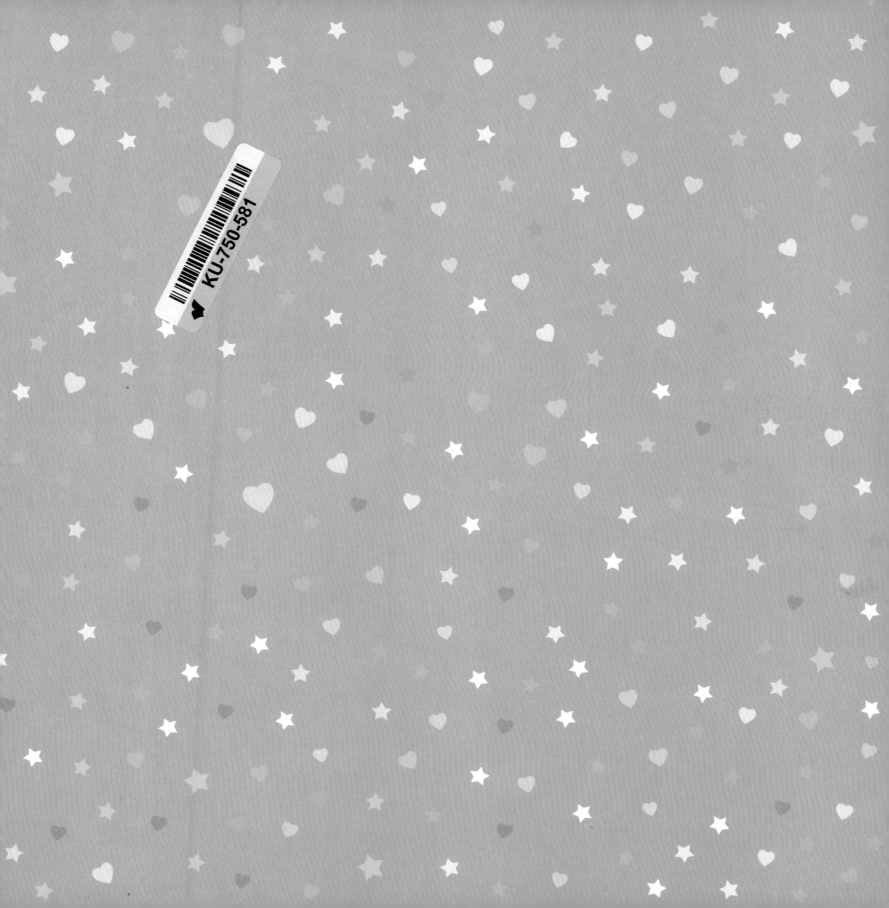

This igloo book belongs to:

_____

igloobooks

*Published in 2014
by Igloo Books Ltd
Cottage Farm
Sywell
NN6 0BJ
www.igloobooks.com*

*SHE001 0114
2 4 6 8 10 9 7 5 3
ISBN 978-1-78197-155-0*

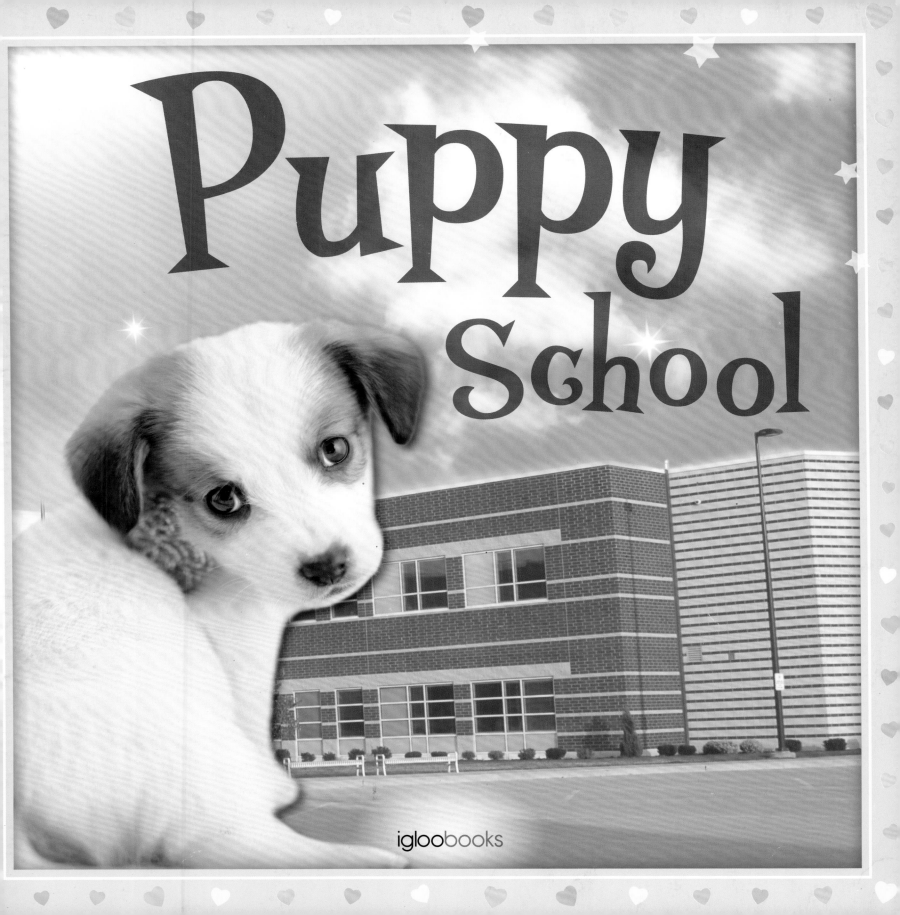

Puppy
School

igloobooks

The puppies are at school and Bossman is in charge for the day. "Today we are going to do something special," he says. "I want you to tell me what you think the best thing about school is."

"I love guitar lessons more than anything," says Regal. "I'm a hound dog."
"Very good, Regal," says Bossman. "I look forward
to hearing a song from you, soon."

"I like playtime the most and I have my lovely, stripy scarf to wear when I'm playing," says Roko. "It's soft and snuggly and keeps me warm when I'm outside in the cold."

"It certainly is a very nice scarf," agrees Bossman.

"We love the library because it's full of books," say Asher and Dozer.
"There are storybooks about puppies and kittens
and all sorts of things," says Asher.
"I want to read every book in the school library."
"Me too," agrees Dozer. "I wonder which one we should read next."

"I love school because I learn lots of amazing things," says Dickens. Dickens is very clever and he loves to read big books and learn lots of amazing things to impress the other puppies. "I love to tell the other puppies what I know. I'm the smartest puppy in school."

"The best thing about school is lunch time," woofs Blake. "All those delicious school dinners make my mouth water! Yum!" "I'm afraid you're going to have to wait a little longer for lunch, Blake," replies Bossman.

Angel is very artistic and Art and Craft is her best lesson at school. "Look at the sparkly stars I made for all my friends," she says, proudly. "They look beautiful, Angel," says Bossman. "Well done!"

Patches and Denver love dancing and are learning a special dance for the school talent show. "We must get the moves right, so we need to practice as much as we can," says Patches. "Wonderful," agrees Bossman. "I look forward to seeing your performance."

Art is Beasley's best lesson. He wants to be a famous painter when he grows up. "I am going to paint a picture for one of my friends," Beasley says. It is messy work, but Beasley doesn't mind at all. He loves getting his paws dirty.

BYRON

"My best thing about school is when we get to write stories and letters," says Watson. "I've written a long letter to my friend, Byron. I can't wait for him to send a letter back to me."

"Well done. Remember to put a stamp on the envelope," says Bossman.

Kylie has been cooking in the school
kitchen for her Cookery class.
"I made you a special cake,
Bossman," says Kylie, happily.
"It looks very tasty,"
says Bossman, licking his lips.
"I'm going to eat it all up
in one go!"

"The best thing about school is being able to use my very own posh briefcase to put everything in," says Archie. He is always very neat and tidy.

CERTIFICATE

Well Done, Beasley

"Drama class is the best thing about school for me," woofs George, excitedly. "I love being able to dress up in all the different clothes and costumes. Do you like my bow tie?"
"It looks perfect, George" says Bossman.

"That's my best lesson, too,"
barks Cosmo. "I found this lovely
old hat to try on.
We're the best-dressed
puppies in school, George.
Just like Bossman."
Bossman is very pleased to see
such well-dressed puppies.

Marshall loves all the fun board games the puppies get to play in the school games club. "I'm the best chess player in school. Does anyone want a game?" asks Marshall. "I am sure that I can win in less than ten moves."

"What about you, Bella and Murphy?" asks Bossman. "What is your best thing about school?" "We love playing catch in the playground," says Bella, excitedly. "Yes, it's our best game," woofs Murphy.

"We love nap time the most," say Connie and Jay, sleepily.
"We need our rest to make sure we enjoy the rest of the day."
"Yes, rest is very important," laughs Bossman.
"As long as you stay awake in your lessons."

"I really like music lessons," barks Deejay, excitedly. "Making music is really good fun and I can listen to it over and over on my music player." "Yes, I like music, too," says Bossman.

The school bell rings, which means it is time for the puppies to go home. "Thank you, Bossman," says Roko, happily. "I can't wait to come back to school again tomorrow."

The puppies had lots of fun in their lesson with Bossman.
Are you as smart as Dickens?
See if you can answer the questions below.

1. Who has a stripy, warm scarf for playing outside?
2. What is Beasley's best lesson at puppy school?
3. Who is Watson writing a letter to?
4. Who likes taking a posh briefcase to school?
5. What is Cosmo wearing?
6. Which little puppies like sleeping at nap time?

1. Roko. 2. Art. 3. Byron. 4. Archie. 5. A top hat and bow tie. 6. Gonnie and Jay.

Goodbye!